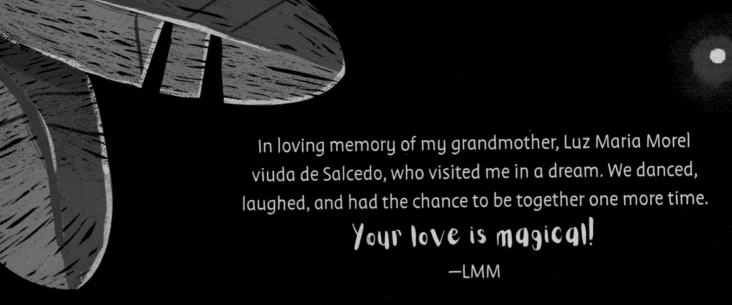

In loving memory of my grandmother, Luz Maria Morel
viuda de Salcedo, who visited me in a dream. We danced,
laughed, and had the chance to be together one more time.
Your love is magical!
—LMM

For the women who raised me between
stories, music, and magic.
—SM

Text by Luz Maria Mack
Illustrations by Stephany Mesa

ISBN 978-1-953859-23-5

Library of Congress Control Number: 2021919950

This is a work of fiction. Names, characters, places and incidents either are the product of the author's imagination
or are used fictitiously. Any resemblance to actual persons, living or dead, events or locales is entirely coincidental.

This book was edited by Tamara Rittershaus and designed by Elizabeth Jayasekera.
The production was supervised by Ceece Kelley.

First edition 2022. Printed and bound in China.

Distributed by Lerner Publishing Group, Inc. 241 First Avenue North Minneapolis, MN 55401 U.S.A

For reading levels and more information, look for this title on www.lernerbooks.com

Soaring Kite Books, LLC
Washington, D.C.
United States of America
www.soaringkitebooks.com

The Secret of the Plátano

story by **Luz Maria Mack**

pictures by **Stephany Mesa**

Soaring Kite Books

Under the full moon,
we will dance.

As the cool night breeze
blows, banana leaves clap
to the beat of tapping feet.

"We have to get the jitters out," Abuela says.

"Sway here,
shake there,
and rustle to the bustle
of the plátanos in the breeze."

The stars light the way
as I follow Abuela's moves.

One step... Two steps...

And jump as we turn!

Nighttime critters circle around us.

We can't see them, but we hear them!

Tiny crickets chitter and chatter
and make us giggle as we wiggle.

Dancing with Abuela is **pure magic.**

I strain my ears to hear the music
that moves Abuela's feet, but only the
chirping of the crickets comes to my ears.

She waves to the night sky and bows to the ground.

She blows kisses to the night winds and whispers a prayer. Her big skirt swoops in circles as she leads our dancing enchantment.

She stands still. "Listen!"

She rests her hands on my little chest.
"Do you hear the drums beating inside you?"

"Why, yes, Abuela, they say **thud, thud, thud.**"

Her dark eyes shine like two black pearls.
She curls her hand behind her ear.

"That's very nice," she says, "very nice indeed.
Do you hear the chitt-chatter of the plátano leaves?"

I close my eyes and listen for it again.

Abuela clutches my hand. "Stand tall, my little one.
Now bow your head to show your respect!

Shh, shh, so you hear
the great secret of the plátanos."

"Abuela, Abuela, can you help me hear
the secret? My tiny ears couldn't hear it!"

Her thin lips curl up in a smile.
"Hmm, I don't know if I can share the
secrets that only my heart knows."

"Please, Abuela, I promise that I will keep its secret **good and true.**"

Abuela nods slowly. "Okay, you have convinced me that you love our plátanos, and that you care for them as much as I do. We dance because under the plátanos, we see the magic of the heavens through its leaves. The plant gives love, and its **love** is the **magic** that helps everything grow."

Now you are small, but one day soon, you will be tall. You, too, are created in **pure perfection** like the golden fruit around us. Let's wave to the moon, the wind, and the plátanos to say goodbye.

Come on, sleepyhead, that's enough dancing for one night."

Love is the magic that
helps everything grow.

A Note from the Author

One of my earliest memories in the Dominican Republic was at my grandmother's house. My cousins and I would run around and play on the front lawn while my aunts and uncles chatted in their wooden rocking chairs on the porch.

Many years later, I dreamed I was a young child in the Dominican Republic. My grandmother was waiting for me under the full moon as the warm air swept us away to a beautiful field.

In my dream, we hugged each other tightly as we often do when I dream of her. She clutched my little hand as I followed her. She knelt to take a good look at me and, with a big grin, assured me all was well. We played all night. My bare feet felt the cool earth as I chased her around, and she made sure to whisk me away in her dancing tradition.

Grateful to have had one more night with her, I wrote *The Secret of the Plátano* in her honor.

— Luz Maria Mack

A Note from the Artist

People say I don't express myself the way other Dominicans do. It's true.

I don't really dance a good merengue, but I know the secrets of the amazing Dominican flavors. I know the smell of the countryside, the river, and what a morivivi (local plant) looks like.

I know that the island of the Dominican Republic is much more than just beautiful beaches. Dominicans, too, are so much more. We are more than the way we speak, look, or dance. We aren't a stereotype; we are different from each other.

I am honored to have illustrated this book with *my* Dominican *sabor* (flavor). I channeled my childhood, running between plátanos in Bonao.

— Stephany Mesa